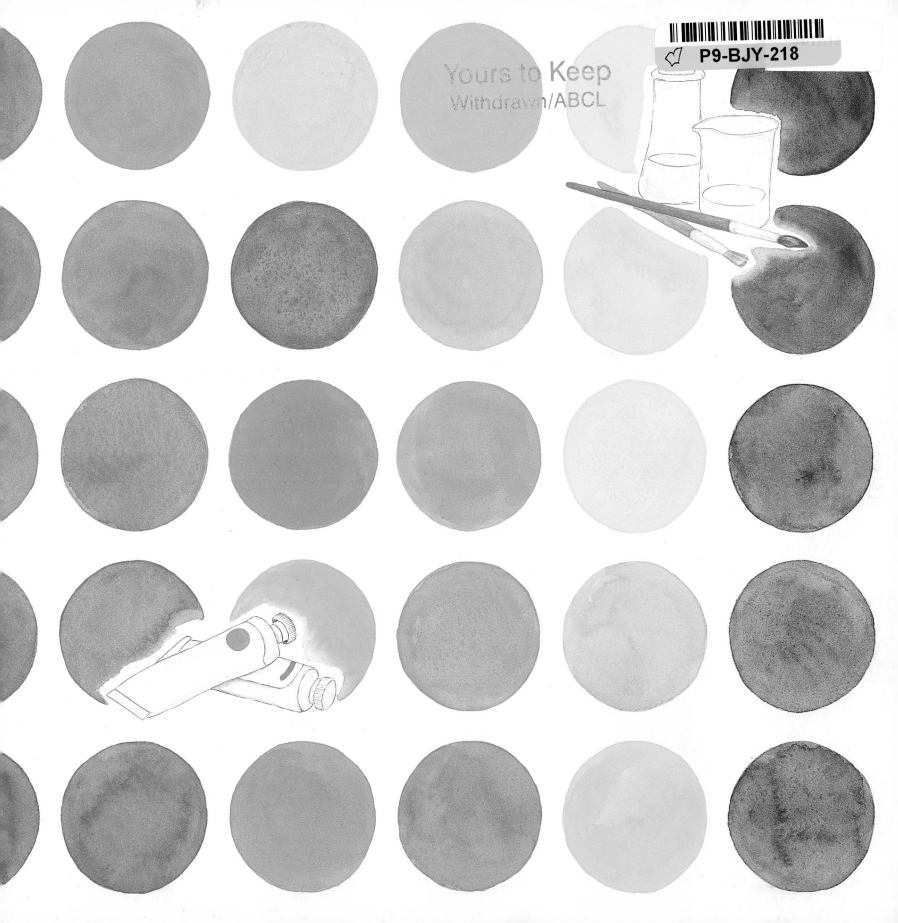

the Art Garden

Penny Harrison & Penelope Pratley

EK

For David, Finlay and Olive.
— P.H.

For Matt, Noah and Psalm.
— P.P.

First published 2018

EK Books
an imprint of Exisle Publishing Pty Ltd
PO Box 864, Chatswood, NSW 2057, Australia
226 High Street, Dunedin, 9016, New Zealand
www.ekbooks.org

A CiP record for this book is available from the National Library of Australia.

ISBN 978-1-925335-59-0

Designed by Big Cat Design
Typeset in Minya Nouvelle 18 on 26pt
Printed in China

This book uses paper sourced under ISO 14001 guidelines from well-managed
forests and other controlled sources.

10 9 8 7 6 5 4 3 2 1

the Art Garden

More than anything, Sadie
wanted to be an artist.

She loved playing with colour and finding patterns in unusual places.

She wanted to capture the little things she saw in the world.

Sadie's best friend, Tom, was an artist.

When Tom painted, Sadie's heart smiled.

She watched his brush dance across the page, swooshing and swirling into shapes and stories.

Sometimes, Sadie felt she was inside the pictures — battling outlaws or swimming with wild swans.

It made her want to be an artist even more.

But what if she couldn't paint as
well as Tom?

What if she couldn't make a picture
come alive the way he did?

One day, Sadie decided to paint a flower.

She picked up the paint brush and the colours slipped and slurped across the page.

But her flower didn't look as beautiful as the real thing.

So, she glared at her brush and went to pick daisies.

Next, she tried to paint a cake.

She picked up the paint brush and the colours splattered and splodged across the page.

But it looked more like a mud pie.

So, she screwed up her paper and
went to plant daffodils.

Tom came to find her.

Together, they romped through the garden.

They chased tadpoles in the shallows.

They baked cakes and decorated them.

Sadie felt her heart was smiling.

But then Tom returned
to his painting.

And Sadie's dream
to be an artist grew
strong again.

So, she picked up the
paint brush and tried to
paint her best friend.

But she tripped on the easel and ended up painting herself.

Sadie wailed. She climbed her favourite tree and refused to come down.

She wondered if she would ever be an artist or if she should just stick to gardening.

For a long time,
Sadie stared down
at the garden.

And then she saw it.

The flowers began
to dance in her
mind, swooshing and
swirling into shapes
and stories.

Sadie clambered
down and picked
up the paint brush
one more time.

She started
scratching
in the dirt.

Next, she scattered
some seeds ...

Pansies for the cakes
she loved to bake.

Violets for the colour
in Tom's paintings.

And forget-me-nots,
because Tom would
always be her best
friend.

Then, she waited.

Slowly, the seeds grew.

Together, Sadie and Tom romped through the garden.

They chased tadpoles in the shallows.

They baked cakes and decorated them.

Each day the seeds grew a little more.

And when Sadie saw her
work of art bloom for the
first time, her heart smiled.

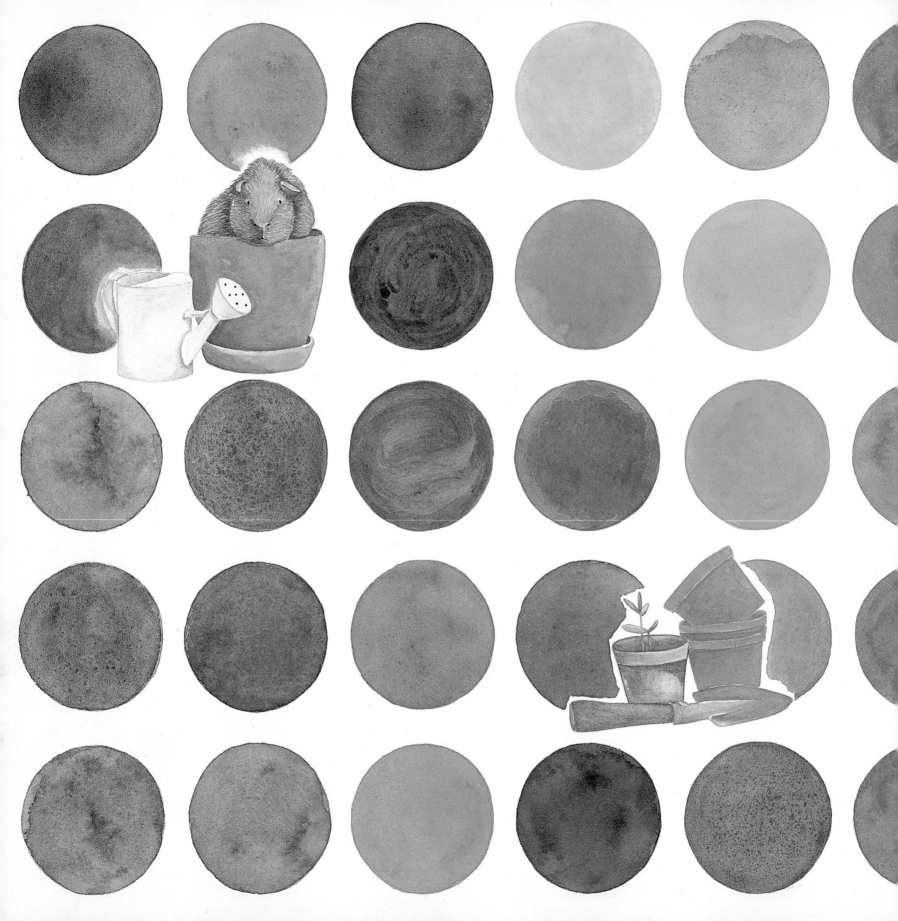